Gabriella

# The Rainbow

award

It is a fine August day
in the Farway Kingdom,
but old King Cole is
not feeling merry. He
goes marching grumpily
around the castle
gardens.

All the elves, pixies and
fairies of the kingdom
hope that they can cheer
him up.

A little elf called Paul goes to ask wise Witch Green for help.

"The king is full of woe because an imp stole his rainbow rose," wise Witch Green tells him. "The rainbow rose gives all the flowers their colour. Without its magic all the flowers have turned white, and yellow flowers are the king's favourite."

"It is the king's birthday soon. I will try to find the rainbow rose and make him happy again. I hope I can do it," says Paul.

And off he goes in search of the rainbow rose.

Paul looks under stones and in the grass. He even looks down a rabbit hole.

"What are you doing?" asks the white rabbit who lives there.

"An imp has stolen the king's rainbow rose," says Paul.

"I will help you look," says the white rabbit.

The pair look everywhere, but they don't find the rainbow rose.

Giving up hope, Paul goes to see wise Witch Green again.

"The king must have his yellow flowers," says Paul. "How can I get them?"

"Your friends may be able to help you," says wise Witch Green.

"How can my friends help?" asks Paul.

"You'll find a way," says the witch.

So Paul goes to see his friend the fairy, who lives in the flower garden.

"The king is sad because an imp has stolen his rainbow rose. Please will you use your fairy magic to make his favourite yellow flowers?" asks Paul.

"I will try, but without the power of the rainbow rose it may not work," explains the fairy.

Next, Paul goes to see the pixies.

"The king is sad because an imp has stolen his rainbow rose," says Paul. "Please use your pixie magic to make a yellow flower for him."

"We will collect the golden rays from the sun, but without the power of the rose it may not work," explain the pixies.

"I will try too," thinks Paul. "I will try to make a yellow flower."

He plants a flower seed in a little pot.

"Please grow," he says. "Because the king is full of woe and you will make him so happy if you do."

He puts the pot out in the August sunshine and waits.

Paul spends the rest of the day talking to the little seed. He tells it how happy King Cole will be when he sees it.

At bedtime, he takes the pot inside and puts it on the windowsill in the light of the moon.

"Please, please grow, little seed," he says.

When morning comes, fairies, pixies and elves from across the kingdom come to give King Cole his birthday presents.

Because of Paul's hard

work, everyone brings
the king's favourite
yellow flowers for him.
Some have been painted.
Some have been made
with magic.

"Yellow flowers. My favourite!" cries the king. "Someone must have found the rainbow rose!"

"We didn't need it after all," says Paul.

The king looks at Paul's flower, then he looks at Paul. "You have made this yellow flower with the magic of love," says the king.

The king's woeful mood goes and he begins to smile.

"We do not need the rainbow rose after all. We just need love. Thank you, Paul. This is the best birthday I have ever had!" says the king.

Because they are happy to see their king smile again, the crowd begins to applaud.

"Hurray for Paul!" they cheer.

## Paul

Describe the character of Paul.

## King Cole

King Cole was 'full of woe'. What does 'woe' mean? Can you describe his mood at the end?

## Witch Green

Why do you think Paul goes to see Witch Green?

## flower

Where did Paul leave the seed at night? Why do you think he did that?

## pixie

How did the pixies say they would make a yellow flower?

## favourite

How many times does the word 'favourite' appear in the story?

## Notes for Parents and Teachers

Popular Rewards Early Readers have been specially created to build young readers' vocabulary, develop their comprehension skills and boost their progress towards independent reading.

★ Make reading fun. Why not read the story and have your child clap when they hear a featured phonics sound, then race to find it on the page?

★ Encourage your child to read aloud to help pick up and resolve any difficulties. As their skills grow, it will also help their fluency and expression.

★ The list of phonics sounds and 'tough and tricky' words will to help consolidate their learning, and the questions will develop comprehension and communication skills.

★ Always keep a positive attitude and focus on your child's achievements. This will help their confidence and build their enjoyment of reading.

ISBN 978-1-78270-232-0

Illustrated by Maureen Bradley



Published by Award Publications Limited,
The Old Riding School, Welbeck, Worksop, S80 3LR

18 1

Printed in Estonia